Rummy
and the
Troglores

By C. J. Kent

GOLDEN FLEECE PRESS

Copyright © 2017 by C. J. Kent

Cover artwork and Chapter headers by Mary Reichelt.

All rights reserved. No part of this publication may be reproduced, distributed, or transmitted in any form or by any means, including photocopying, recording, or other electronic or mechanical methods, without the prior written permission of the publisher, except in the case of brief quotations embodied in critical reviews and certain other noncommercial uses permitted by copyright law. For permission requests, write to the publisher, addressed "Attention: Permissions Coordinator," at the address below.

Golden Fleece Press
PO Box 1464,
Centreville, VA 20122
www.goldenfleecepress.com

Special discounts are available on quantity purchases by corporations, associations, and others. For details, contact the publisher at the address above.

Epub ISBN 13:   978-1-942195-49-8
Mobi ISBN 13:   978-1-942195-50-4
Pdf ISBN 13:   978-1-942195-48-1
Print ISBN 13:   978-1-942195-47-4

Printed in the United States of America

First Edition

10 9 8 7 6 5 4 3 2 1

Dedication

To Family—
Ann for the inspiration & continuous loving support;
Oliver for sparking the story that became what you now hold;
William for the snuggly slumber that gave me the time to
create.

CHAPTER ONE

Rummy barked in alarm.

He stuck his golden, white-tipped nose deep into the hole he had found in the backyard and began rooting furiously. He paddled his front paws at the hole, trying to widen it so that he could tunnel through. It was not working, but he imagined it could. That he could fit. He could see himself corkscrewing through in search of the tiny creatures that had made the hole: the troglores.

Rummy raised his head for air, chunks of icy dirt and half-melted snow fell off his nose, and he sounded the alarm again. *Bark! Bark-Bark-Bark!*

A man exited the house's sliding glass door and shouted. "Rummy! Here boy! Quit tearing up the yard!"

Toby, a small boy of six years of age or so stepped out and joined the man, his father. "He's at it again?"

Rummy looked over at them both, but quickly turned his attention back to the hole. Dig. Dig. Dig. Rummy knew Toby and his father thought Rummy was being bad, but he was really trying to protect them. If he could just get to the troglores...

The father looked down at his son, his disheveled light brown hair shining in the afternoon sun. "Yeah, at it again. Why do you think that dog keeps digging up the yard, Toby?"

"I don't know, Dad."

Even though furiously digging, Rummy heard the exchange and felt confused. Toby knew about the troglores. He and Toby talked about the vile digging creatures all the time. Well, Toby talked and Rummy listened. Toby told him how they were the scourge of the underground world, seeking to bring the above-ground world into the darkness of dirt, tunneling through the neighborhoods in search of new conquests and, worst of all, food.

In fact, Toby's stories were the reason Rummy had started patrolling the backyard night and day. Toby's stories were the reason Rummy had known there was trouble when he spotted the first hole in the snow the other day.

Now there were more. Dozens more.

If he could just widen one enough to squeeze into, he could find the nasty little critters and maybe, just maybe, put a stop to their apparent plot to take over the backyard.

"Well," sighed Toby's dad, "go get him, clean him up, and yourself afterwards. Dinner's soon."

Toby trotted out into the yard. He clapped to get Rummy's attention and grabbed at his collar. "Come on, boy. They're not there. Come on, let's get you cleaned up."

Toby led Rummy back to the sliding glass door and picked up a damp towel that his father put out for him. He ran the towel gently across Rummy's dirty muzzle and paws, pulling chunks of frozen ground and ice from his toes.

Rummy had been a present to the Ferguson family shortly after Toby had been born. It seemed like a poor idea, a baby and a golden retriever puppy at the same time, but Rummy took to Toby fast. Late night feedings—Rummy was there. Bath times—

Rummy splashed along. First day at school—Rummy helped walk Toby home.

Now the two were inseparable, always playing and always taking care of each other. "You did good, boy. You kept an eye out. Dad doesn't understand, but I do. You want to find them, but I keep telling you, the troglores are long gone. They don't like winter. They're hibernating deep underground, where it's warm. Those holes, they're from squirrels, Rummy. Just squirrels."

Rummy loved his master, but he knew Toby was wrong. Squirrels did not make holes like that. Squirrels didn't leave smells behind like that. Squirrels weren't trying to take over the above-ground world. The troglores were—no matter what Toby said.

The next day, while Toby was at school, and everyone else was at work, Rummy patrolled the sliding glass door to the backyard, watching for any signs of activity.

The sun slowly peeked out from behind a curtain of gray clouds, and began melting what little snow was left on the ground. As that cover of white disappeared, Rummy saw what he feared—holes. Every few feet, divots and dents and holes across the yard: under the trees, by the patio, next to the sandbox—everywhere.

By late afternoon, Rummy was agitated and hoarse from non-stop barking. He felt crazed. How were the troglores doing this in the day? Their eyes and skin were supposed to be too sensitive to sunlight. This should not be possible! And the cold? Even with the sun warming the day, the temperature should have been well cold enough to halt their activity. At least from the stories Toby had told him.

Toby had heard the barking when he and his mom pulled the car into the driveway, so he rushed inside to let Rummy out figuring he needed to go to the bathroom. But, Rummy did not need to go, he just needed out to have a chance to stop the troglores.

As soon as Toby opened the sliding glass door, Rummy bounded out into the yard, barking with each step. He circled the yard several times, surveying the damage. He counted ten new holes since yesterday. Ten! The one over by the oak tree was the biggest by far. He headed to that, and immediately began digging. Within just a few scoops of dirt, the sides of the hole gave way, and Rummy began to fall in!

Before he slipped completely through, Rummy heard Toby cry out, "Rummy! No!!"

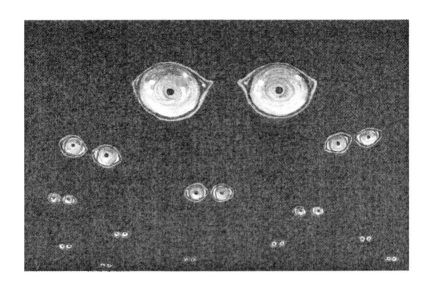

CHAPTER TWO

Rummy pawed at the sides of the large hole, but could not stop himself from falling. He could not even muster the lung power to bark back to Toby in response. He fell rapidly, sliding deeper down the hole, past spindly and gnarled roots, and veins of red clay that zig-zagged along the sides of the hole.

Down, down, down Rummy slid.

He felt a strange stretching sensation, as if his tail was being left behind while his head fell further and further in. And, then, *SNAP!* The back of his body caught up with the front, and all of him was finally ejected from the other side of the hole.

Rummy was a tangle of flailing legs, but quickly righted himself onto all fours. The first thing he noticed was the awful sour, wet stench of troglore. Then, he noticed *eyes*. All around him tiny, beady, evil, red eyes.

Rummy locked his stance, the hair along his neck and back raising in alarm. He started growling and snarling, first out of the fear that had been driving him mad all day, and then out of anger. These were the dirty, scary troglores behind it all; the invaders that kept digging up his yard.

There were three standing before Rummy, about a foot high, no taller than him, but every bit as hideous as Toby had once described. They all snarled back at Rummy, baring their thick, pointy yellow teeth. It was a tinny, hollow snarl that hurt Rummy's ears. Their jet-black fur was all matted, clumped with clay and dirt. Each sat up on their hind haunches, slashing their front paws in the air at Rummy, showing off their sharp, curled digging nails with each swipe.

Growling, Rummy quickly scanned his surroundings. He was in a vast, underground cavern. The air was stuffy, thick and hot. Pillars of dirt stretched from floor to ceiling, seemingly keeping the world from collapsing in. Torches hung along the pillars and walls, flickering faint light across the entire cavern. Scratches were carved into the dirt everywhere, making it evident that whole thing had been dug out by paw—troglore paw.

Just how far, and how deep, had he fallen?

Panic flooded him, and he fought to keep from shaking. He had wanted this, but he had been in a frenzy above ground. Now that he stood face to face with the creatures, he didn't know what to do. He had no idea where he was. He had no idea what was going to happen next. He had every reason to be afraid.

But he did not want to be afraid. Shaking in front of the troglores would not help. He did the only thing that he could to chase both the fear and the snarling creatures away: he switched from growling to barking. Loudly.

BARK! BARK! BARK-BARK-BARK-BARK!

The troglores flinched, and stepped back; clearly startled by the loud noise and its endless echo in the cavern.

Energized, Rummy seized the moment to press his new-found advantage and charged.

The troglores dropped to all fours and ran, sounding off in non-stop chirps. Rummy started off chasing them around one of the larger pillars in the cavern. After several passes around, the creatures wised up and ran sideways into a large, off-shoot tunnel.

Rummy chased after them.

The troglores were fast for such small creatures. They dashed over the rough terrain with ease. Rummy pushed himself, jumping and dashing across the uneven, rough ground. He barked the entire time.

He tried desperately to keep up, but the underground dwellers were more familiar with the environment, and faster than Rummy. The deeper into the tunnel he ran, the smaller it became, and soon Rummy was ducking the tree roots and sharp rocks that poked out of the tunnel walls at odd angles.

When he realized the troglores had disappeared, he slowed to a trot, and stopped. He was all alone. And, worse, it was much darker than in the cavern; there were no torches lighting his way.

A few whines escaped Rummy's throat.

He was beyond lost. He had been so focused on catching the vicious critters that he had no idea if he had stayed within the same tunnel or taken a curve and gone down some off-shoot. More whines bubbled up from the back of his throat and echoed all around him. He whipped his head around, considering if he should turn around and try to go back to the cavern, see if he could find the hole he fell through, or just press on to see what was ahead.

And then, in the distance, he heard a faint yet familiar noise.

Bark! Bark! Bark!

Another dog! Rummy headed off towards the sound, but slowed when he realized he couldn't be sure if he was following the bark or the echo. He closed his eyes and let his ears lead the way.

Bark! bark! bark!

There it was again, but fainter than before. He turned around and trotted back the way he came. He passed several smaller side tunnels, each carrying a humid breeze with its own host of smells and strange sounds, but not the barking.

Eventually he came to a small side tunnel that did carry the barking. Cautious, he slipped in and traveled on, as the barking grew louder and mixed with what sounded like water.

CHAPTER THREE

After several minutes, the tunnel opened into a cliff overlooking a new cavern. Rushing water echoed in the chamber, which was all but flooded. A large, lone, flat rock jutted out of the water, just a few feet from the cliff. A small, but very loud barking dog sat atop the rock.

"BARK! BARK! BARK!"

"Hello?!" Rummy called down.

Startled, the tiny white Mexican Chihuahua turned around and noticed Rummy. "Oh, thank goodness," he called up to Rummy with glee. "I'm stuck. Please help!"

"How? What can I do?"

"Get some rope, anything to help me get up there."

It was a valid request, but not only did Rummy not have rope, he had not seen any evidence of anything similar back in the tunnel. "Rope? From where?"

The tiny dog barked excitedly. "I don't know, *amigo*, but the water is pouring in faster, and the level keeps rising, so any help here would be much appreciated."

"But I—"

"Look around. There has to be something!"

Rummy felt trapped, he wanted to help but could not think of what to do. Maybe the dog was right, maybe there was something around. Rummy turned and went back up the tunnel, this time not focused on what was in front of him, but what was all around him. Dirt, rocks, roots, more dirt, tiny rocks, big rocks, big root, more—*wait a moment*, he thought—roots!

Rummy darted back and forth in the tunnel searching for a large root, one big enough to use as a bridge for the tiny dog to come up from the rock. But it was no good, they were all either too short or too thin and spindly.

Rummy ran back to the tunnel's end, and shouted down to the dog. "I can't find anything. Nothing is big enough or strong enough to use."

"Yip! Yip!" exclaimed the dog. "There has to be something, anything to pull me up!"

Pull, thought Rummy. That was it! He ran back to where he had seen the largest root and started digging and gnawing. Within a few minutes, he had dug out, and chewed free from the wall, a large hunk of root. He raced back to the tunnel's entrance and threw one end down to the dog. It was long enough that one end crashed into the water below, and the other end stayed by Rummy's side.

Rummy called down, "jump in and bite on – I'll pull you up!"

The Chihuahua wagged his tail furiously, stomped his back legs several times, as if gathering courage, and then jumped into the water. He swam to the root and let out a water-logged bark before growling and biting down on the root. Rummy did the same, biting hard on the root at his end, and then started tugging and pulling in short, rapid bursts.

After a few good pulls from Rummy, for a brief moment, the Chihuahua spun around as he dangled in the air from the root. But Rummy kept pulling and before long the tiny white dog was scrambling up the mouth of the tunnel and running to meet Rummy.

CHAPTER FOUR

The Chihuahua jumped and ran circles around Rummy, who sat panting next to the half-chewed root. "That was incredible! Thank you! My name is Shorty. That was amazing!"

Rummy stood, dazed still from the exertion. He yawned to exercise his jaw. "Pleased to meet you Shorty, my name is Rummy."

"Rummy. Rummy. Where are you from, Rummy, and how did you get here?"

"I arrived in a cavern, back that way." Rummy nodded his head backwards. "I had been chasing some troglores down this hole and—"

"Suddenly found yourself in a huge cavern with torches? Yeah, same thing happened to me."

"Then how'd you end up down there?"

"Running without looking. The troglore I chased started chasing me when I arrived. I took off at a fast clip and didn't realize I was about to run out of road. Next thing I knew, I was flying right out of the tunnel and into the water. I think I made a big splash for such a tiny dog!" The Chihuahua laughed at his own joke.

Shorty continued, "But the water was much deeper than I could handle. I paddled over to the rock for safety. That was several days ago, but now, thanks to that strong bite of yours, I'm back in this tunnel. We should head back, see if we can get out of this place."

Rummy agreed, and both dogs took off running. But getting back to the cavern was easier said than done. Rummy was all turned around and Shorty had no idea how to get back, either. The two kept getting lost in off-shoot tunnels, and spent a lot of time backtracking trying to stay on the right path.

"My sense of smell is all scrambled down here," said Rummy, as he wished he could just use his nose to lead him back to a way home.

"*Si*," agreed Shorty. "All I can smell is troglore. I'll be glad to get home to breathe clean air."

"Are there many of them where you're from?" Rummy asked as they trotted.

"*Si*, that was part of the reason why I went down the hole. To stop them from digging up, sure, but also to see if I could capture one and show it we mean business." Shorty made a thrusting chomp motion as if he was biting at an invisible troglore.

Rummy shuddered at the thought of biting one. If they smelled that bad, how must they taste? "That's pretty bold of you."

"Says the dog who pulled me up from my watery doom!"

Rummy tried to brush off the compliment; he didn't think he deserved it. "That was nothing. That was a good idea, by the way, having me pull you up."

Shorty chuckled. "My idea? I may have said pull, but you're the one who found a root to do it with. Admit it, you're one *valiente* dog, *mi amigo*."

Rummy looked down, and said thanks softly. Then he changed the subject. "Do you think the troglores dug all this out, or found it?"

"*Si*, I think they dug it all out. The way I hear it, the troglores have been doing a lot of digging, searching for centuries for a lost city of theirs. There's this old trog hunter, in the jungle near where I live, and he says that within this lost city is a special fire gem that would give them the strength to roam the surface once more."

Rummy envisioned Shorty sitting before an old dog in the jungle, immersed in stories of the nasty critters, much like the way Rummy sat before Toby listening to his wild tales.

"Does this hunter know how to stop the troglores?"

"Dogs. He says we are the key, the frontline of defense."

"Why us?"

"Our pack mentality and loyalty to humans means we can easily assemble, protect and attack. And the troglores know it. I think that's why they tease us and get us to follow them down their holes. They want to get rid of us, I think. I hear they are drawing as many down here as they can. I've heard rumors from others of dog prisons."

"Others? So, you know other dogs who have seen and fought them?"

"It is almost common knowledge where I come from, among us dogs, that they exist. In fact, many believe that a great war with the troglores is coming."

"No one believes me, or my master, where I am from."

"Then it is up to you to get home to warn the others."

Rummy did not like the sound of that. He didn't want to mobilize any great dog armies or convince others of this nightmare he had fallen into. He just wanted to go home and curl up with Toby. He wanted to be done with this underground adventure.

By the time the two made it back to the cavern they were exhausted. Cautiously, Rummy and Shorty walked into the open space. "Do you remember where you fell in?" asked Shorty.

Rummy scanned the cavern and nodded off to the far direction. "Over there, I think. Hard to say for sure. Do you remember?"

"No, I came through so fast I barely had time to realize I was even in a cavern."

"There are so many holes in the walls," Rummy said. "Where do you think they all go?

How many backyards are these things digging into?"

Shorty did not respond. Rummy supposed he did not need him to. It was clear now that the troglores were looking to get into every backyard, or more, that they could.

Shorty started walking the length of the cavern walls, sniffing. Rummy followed suit moving along the opposite side. He struggled to smell past the stench of troglore. Eventually he started to pick up the faint scent of other dogs, but never his own scent, or Shorty's.

After several minutes Shorty called out. "Here, over here! I think this might be where you fell in."

Rummy dashed over. There was certainly a lot of kicked up dirt, which made sense given how he had squared off with troglores when he arrived. And he did smell himself heavily in the area. "I think this is the right spot," he said. "But, there are five holes here along the wall, how do I know which one I came through?"

"You keep sniffing, while I keep checking for mine. But, worst case, you jump through one of those and you get that much closer to home. With them being clustered so closely together like that, I think they must all lead to the same general area."

Rummy only barely heard Shorty as he immersed himself in sniffing. He pawed up the wall, stretching to reach his nose to the holes, each of which was several feet up from the floor. He was so focused on identifying which one smelled the most like him that he missed what was rushing towards him.

The troglore hit Rummy with the force of a pack of wild dogs, barreling into him and throwing him several feet sideways. It took a moment for Rummy to register what had happened, and in that space of time, the troglore was charging again like a rabid bull. Rummy barked ferociously. He hoped to scare it off, but also to alert Shorty that the creatures had arrived!

CHAPTER FIVE

The barking did not stop the charging troglore, so Rummy threw himself forward to tackle and get the upper paw. The two collided and wrestled each other to the ground. Rummy snapped his teeth and pushed with his legs, trying to fight it off as it slashed at Rummy with its sharp digging nails. Over the noise of his own growls and barks, and the skittering squeals of the troglore, Rummy heard Shorty yell that more were coming.

Rummy managed to flip himself over on top of the tiny dirt-dwelling monster he was wrestling with and was trying to figure out what to do next, when the troglores that Shorty warned of arrived. They quickly surrounded Rummy, each jerking and tugging at parts of his four-legged body until he was completely immobilized. They pulled him off the one troglore, and started skittering in their language, Troglorese.

Rummy could understand people, talk with other dogs and cats, and even sometimes get the gist of other kinds of animals, but these underground dwelling creatures were too foreign for him. However, in this instance, Rummy didn't have to speak Troglorese to know what was happening. He had been captured. He was their prisoner.

The troglores began dragging Rummy back towards the middle of the cavern, Rummy howled in frustration and fear. He struggled to turn to see if Shorty had also been captured, but neither heard nor saw his new friend. Then, right in front of the cluster of tunnels that led back to Rummy's home, the troglores stopped and stood perfectly still.

A shadow fell across Rummy. A new troglore arrived. He looked similar to the others, eyes wide and blood red, fur black as the dead of night, but there was something different about this one. This troglore was taller and his fur was coarse and completely slicked back. His snout and teeth were less prominent and he seemed more aware and calm. He also had a tiny sliver of red crystal hanging around his neck, dangling from a rope that was woven from the roots that grew all throughout the tunnels.

More than just his appearance, this troglore seemed like the grown up of the bunch. The others were excited, clamoring for the new one's attention. It was clear that this was not just any regular troglore, this was a leader.

The leader looked at Rummy and bared his teeth, but did not attack. The Leader wanted Rummy to know that he was in charge, not Rummy. The troglore made a scratchy noise, different from the chirping he and the other troglores had made earlier. He grabbed at the red crystal around his neck, and continued speaking – but this time, to Rummy's shock, he understood scraps of what was said through the skittering chirps.

"You…much…trouble…dog."

Rummy quaked with fear. He felt like he was being lectured before receiving a punishment. The only question was, what was the punishment going to be?

The leader stared straight into Rummy's eyes. "All…dogs…to us…you…but…warrior."

Warrior? Did the leader just call him a warrior? Rummy did not consider himself a warrior, but he was happy to let the leader think that was the case. In fact, the idea of it gave Rummy a burst of confidence; it was just what he needed to stop shaking.

Rummy turned the word over in his mind and started to pretend that he was a warrior. He wanted to think like a warrior. What would a warrior do? How would he act?

He barked and growled and tried to speak slowly himself. "Dogs of my country are fierce trog hunters, we will beat you back." Rummy didn't believe a word of it, but the leader did not know that to be the case.

"How…dogs…army…number?"

It was then that Rummy finally heard Shorty. Rumbling up from behind the leader, and heading straight to Rummy, the tiny Chihuahua bellowed a large BARK! and exclaimed, "Get home, warn your family, tell them the troglores are coming." Shorty slammed head-first into the leader, tumbling him into Rummy with such speed that both the leader and Rummy went flying up and back into the air, straight into one of the holes.

Rummy felt himself get sucked into and through the hole, alongside with the leader, and he heard Shorty follow up his war cry with, "Now we are even, *amigo*—good luck!"

CHAPTER SIX

Unlike before, where Rummy fell through the hole smoothly, this time he tumbled, bumped, bounced, and jerked his way through. He was aware each step of the way that he was not alone—the leader was traveling with him. He felt the funny stretching sensation again and then, before he knew it, he was falling through the side of a cracked concrete wall and onto the floor of a large, dark storm drain.

A trickle of water passed beneath him, soaking his back. He heard the leader troglore thump into the tunnel as well. Rummy scrambled up and moved backwards to turn and face the creature who had been his captor just moments ago. But the leader was not standing on his feet, he was not lunging to attack or even scrambling to retreat— he was just lying there, silent.

It looked as if he had injured himself.

Rummy growled, his voice deep and thick. He was not sure if he should back down or press an attack. The troglores were evil creatures, and it appeared as if he had the advantage with the leader vulnerable in front of him. This was his chance to safeguard his home and neighborhood for good. Rummy felt a sudden urge to lunge and strike the monster, but he could not.

The troglores *were* evil, but despite having been a prisoner just moments ago, they were not a threat at that moment. Which meant Rummy was not scared—cautious and aware, yes, but not angry and scared.

Rummy stood back and barked, testing to see if he could shock the leader awake. He stirred, glanced around, and quickly locked eyes with Rummy. The leader rolled out a guttural noise, similar to a growl, and began to slowly roll back and forth. Soon he was on his feet, all fours, facing off with Rummy. The leader squeaked and reached up to his chest below his neck but found only air. The rope and the red crystal were gone!

Was that what enabled Rummy to understand him? Had that been a piece of the fire gem?

The troglore leader seemed to realize the same thing and abandoned trying to talk. He checked his surroundings once more, as if to make sure that they were alone, and then reached out a paw palm up, bowing his head slightly.

It was not a friendly gesture, but it was not aggressive either. Rummy wasn't sure how to interpret it so he tried to think like a warrior. And, as a warrior dog, Rummy thought it was almost like an act of…respect.

Rummy did not think for one second that he had stopped the troglores, that they would go away forever, but rather that the leader was looking to save face, regroup to dig another day in another yard.

Before Rummy could think of what to do next, a rumble echoed into the tunnel and the hole behind the leader ejected three snarling, angry troglores. They all hit the ground on their feet, ready to attack. Two took a protective position beside their lord and master, while the other made a move towards Rummy.

The leader lashed out a paw and pulled the attacking troglore down to the ground. He skittered out a burst of chirps, and the two protectors grabbed at the downed troglore and pulled him away from Rummy. The leader chittered out more squeaks, with a few clicks, and the other troglores lowered their heads. They obediently climbed back into the tunnel hole and vanished.

Rummy stared hard at the leader. He returned Rummy's look and nodded respectfully. It was, as far as Rummy was concerned, the admission he had thought: *You win, just go and we'll call it a truce— we'll leave your home alone.*

Never once taking his eye of Rummy, the troglore leader backed into the hole and, using his powerful arms, pulled the edge of the hole in around him until both he and the hole had vanished.

Rummy was suddenly all alone. The troglores were gone. Their tunnel was gone. And now the path back to Shorty was also gone. He whimpered. The large storm drain he was in felt much smaller and much darker than it was.

But as he looked around, he saw a disc of white light a few hundred yards away. Sunlight. The entrance to the drain. He gave one last good growling bark at the spot where the troglores disappeared, backed away a few steps, and then trotted towards the light.

Rummy emerged from the storm drain tired, but feeling good. Rummy had shown those underground monsters that he was not going to stand for any invaders in his yard. He had protected himself and his human family. He had been the warrior dog that the leader had suggested.

Dusk was settling in and tiny snowflakes were starting to fall.

He sniffed the air for a scent of home, looked around, and realized where he was. The tunnel had run west underneath the neighborhood, towards a nearby park. He was just a few blocks from home. In the distance, he could hear Toby calling his name. *"Rummy!!!!"*

Rummy smiled, and ran off towards home sounding off with a happy bark. He was anxious to get home, see Toby and have a nice, hot bath.

Toby was ecstatic to see him. After a huge welcome home hug, Toby's father proclaimed both Rummy and Toby too dirty for dinner and marched both to the tub for a bath. Afterwards, all clean, the two spent the rest of the time before dinner staring out the window at the falling snowflakes. Rummy had no concern of new holes that evening.

Later that night, after Toby's mother and father tucked their son into bed, they tried to take Rummy downstairs with them but Toby refused to let Rummy out of his sight.

Eventually, Toby's parents gave in and left Rummy in Toby's room. Once the door was closed, Toby launched into a chain of fanciful troglore stories, making up wild tales about what happened to Rummy. They were elaborate accounts of giant fire spewing troglores, stone towers, knights in armor, underground lava monsters, and more.

"And I bet you attacked all of them, didn't ya boy? You growled and bit and tore into them, fighting your way home."

Rummy yawned, and curled in closer to the boy. Toby was bouncing off the walls with excitement. He had watched Rummy fall into the Trog hole and it had obviously scared him. And while Toby felt better that Rummy was back, it seemed to Rummy that Toby was still incredibly anxious and scared. It was as if Toby's imagination was stepping in to help deal with it all. Rummy realized it was something that happened a lot, and when it did, Rummy would just share the fear and soak in every word Toby said.

But, on this night, Rummy did not. Not because the truth was so far off from Toby's wild tales of brave knights and super scary troglores, but because Rummy had an idea of what he was up against. And, more importantly, Rummy knew how he would react.

Rummy was a warrior now. And that word, that experience of hearing and seeing himself as one, gave Rummy a sense of confidence. He was scared, sure, but he knew he could protect himself and his family. He would find other dogs and warn them, because sooner or later the troglores would be back.

And when they did come back, maybe, just maybe, after Rummy was done fending them off, he could get a chance to dive back into the underground world and find his pal Shorty.

The End
(Well, until next time...)

About the Author

C. J. Kent started his writing career over thirty years ago, when he first put pencil to lined paper to practice his upper and lower case letters. Cursive writing proved difficult, so he retired to focus on getting older, getting a job, getting married, and having a family. But the dream of being a writer never left him.

Over time, he found himself augmenting his kids' nightly bedtime reading routine with stories of his own. With much encouragement from his wife and friends, he eventually decided that it was time to come out of retirement.

He spends his days and nights typing away in the suburbs of Northern Virginia with his wife, two kids, mouthy cat, and crazy dog that bears no resemblance to Rummy whatsoever. When not working or writing, he blogs about nonsense—books, movies, and pancakes—and shares pictures of his life and the dog that is not Rummy.